A CHRISTMAS CAROL

CHARLES DICKENS

Ebenezer Scrooge sat in his office counting his money. It was Christmas Eve, and seven years to the day that his greedy partner, Jacob Marley, had died.

Bob Cratchit, the clerk, was busily working in the cold, cramped office. His coat and scarf were threadbare and worn.

A group of carol singers began their first sweet song under the window.

"Bah, humbug! Go away!" bellowed Scrooge. He turned angrily to Bob Cratchit. "I suppose you'll want all day tomorrow?" he asked.

"If it's convenient, sir," said Bob.

"Well, it's not," growled Scrooge, "but go ahead. Just be here all the earlier the next day."

Scrooge went to the cold, dark house where he lived all alone. He put two lumps of coal on the fire and sat down to a bowl of gruel.

Suddenly, he heard bells ringing all over the house. They stopped as quickly as they had begun, and Scrooge heard a loud, clanking noise. It was as if someone were dragging a heavy chain up the stairs.

Scrooge stared in surprise as the ghost of Jacob Marley walked straight through the closed door. He was wrapped in a chain made of steel cash boxes, keys and padlocks.

The ghost gave a fearful cry and said, "Look at me, Ebenezer. That is the chain I made for myself in life. All I cared about was money. But your chain is even longer, and it is still growing. Be warned, friend Ebenezer. Tonight you will be visited by three spirits who will show you the way to keep from becoming like me. Listen to them well."

Marley's ghost floated through the window and out into the bleak, black night. Terrified, Scrooge went straight to bed.

On the stroke of one, he woke up. The room glowed with an eerie light and Scrooge found himself staring at another ghost.

"I am the Spirit of Christmas Past. Your past, Ebenezer Scrooge," it droned. "Rise and come with me."

The ghost took Scrooge's hand and they floated through the wall into a village street.

"I lived here as a child," cried Scrooge.

A happy crowd of boys was playing in the snow and calling "Merry Christmas" to passersby.

Scrooge peeped in the schoolroom window. He saw one little boy sitting all alone, reading a book.

"Nobody likes him," said the ghost. "The others don't want to play with him. All he wants is to make a fortune. He doesn't care about making friends."

"That is me, when I was nine years old," said Scrooge tearfully. "Oh, how terrible!"

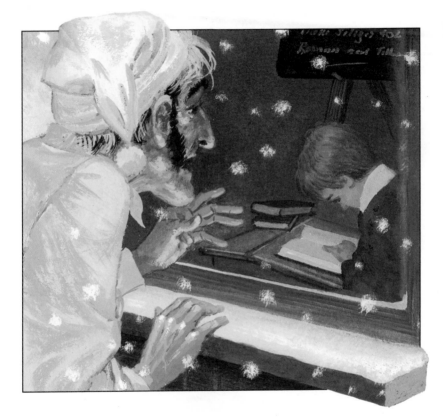

Suddenly they were inside a small cottage. They saw a pretty young girl sitting at a tiny writing table.

"Oh, Ghost," cried Scrooge. "That's Belle. I planned to marry her once, a long time ago."

The girl could not see them. She was trying to write a letter through her tears. Scrooge peered over her shoulder.

. . . You see, dear Ebenezer, there is something you love more than me — money. I hope that you will remember me when you are rich. Goodbye.

Your own sweetheart,

Belle

"Oh, I can't stand it! I can't change the past," cried Scrooge. "Oh, please. Take me home, Ghost."

As soon as he said the words, Scrooge was back in his bed. Exhausted, he fell asleep.

Once again, the clock struck one. This time the light seemed to be coming from the next room. A merry voice called, "Come in, come in!"

Scrooge opened the door and saw a fat, jolly ghost in a robe trimmed with fur. He was wearing a crown of holly on his head.

"I am the Spirit of Christmas Present," he said. "Touch my robe."

Church bells rang everywhere. People dressed in their Sunday best hurried past, wishing each other a merry Christmas.

The ghost took Scrooge to the small house where Bob Cratchit lived with his wife and their five children. Mrs. Cratchit was cooking a small, skinny goose, a dish of potatoes, applesauce and a tiny plum pudding.

Bob hurried into the room. He was carrying his youngest son, Tiny Tim, on his shoulders. The boy was crippled.

"They are very poor," said the ghost. "If Tim doesn't get enough to eat, he will die. Then poor Bob's heart will break."

No one complained about the small size of the dinner. When they had finished, Bob proposed a toast. "To Ebenezer Scrooge, who pays my wages and so provided this meal."

"God bless him!" cried Tiny Tim. "God bless us, every one!"

But Mrs. Cratchit said, "Humph. I won't drink to that cold, stingy man."

Scrooge's face dropped. "Please take me home, Ghost," he pleaded.

But the ghost had vanished. And once again the clock struck one. Scrooge saw a hooded figure gliding toward him through the mist. Its black cloak hid everything but one thin, white hand.

"I fear you," trembled Scrooge. "I know who you are. You are the Spirit of Christmas Yet to Come."

Instead of answering, the ghost pointed to a new grave in the cemetery where they were standing. Its cheap headstone had two words carved on it: EBENEZER SCROOGE.

"Oh, no, Ghost!" cried Scrooge. "I'll be different. I will! I will!"

Scrooge woke up trembling. He was in his own room, in his own bed. And best of all, he was not dead!

"Oh," he said to himself, laughing and crying all at the same time. "I don't know what to do first!"

He opened the window and called to a boy in the street below, "What day is this?"

"Why, Christmas Day, of course, sir."

"Thank heavens, I haven't missed it," said Scrooge. "Now, boy, take this money and go to the poultry shop. I want you to buy that big prize turkey and ask them to take it to Bob Cratchit's house. But don't say who sent it. And you can keep the change for yourself.

Scrooge dressed himself in his best clothes. He went to church for the first time in years. Then he walked through the streets calling, "Merry Christmas!" to everyone he saw.

Scrooge went to his office very early the next day. He wanted to arrive before Bob Cratchit. And he did. Bob Cratchit was late for work! Scrooge pretended to be very angry.

"What do you mean by coming in here at this time of day?" he growled.

"I'm very sorry, sir," said Bob, afraid of losing his job. "I had a wonderful Christmas. The most amazing thing happened . . . but, I promise this won't happen again, sir."

"I can promise you it won't," said Scrooge, trying to hide a smile. "I won't stand for this sort of thing any longer."

And with that, Scrooge leapt from his stool and surprised Bob by giving him a dig in the ribs.

"I'm going to raise your salary, Bob Cratchit! Merry Christmas! Stoke the fire and put on some more coal. This afternoon, we'll talk about how I can help you and your splendid family."

So Tiny Tim did not die, and no more ghosts visited Scrooge in the middle of the night. In fact, for the rest of his life, people said that Ebenezer Scrooge knew how to celebrate Christmas better than any man or woman alive.

May that be said of all of us as well. And so, as Tiny Tim observed, God bless us, every one!

A *Christmas Carol*, originally published in 1843, was the first and best-loved in a series of Christmas stories by Charles Dickens. Considered by many to be the greatest English novelist of all time, the inspiration for much of his fiction came from a difficult and painful childhood. His father was imprisoned for debt and, at the age of 12, Dickens was sent to work in a blacking factory. Later he worked as an office boy, then a county reporter, then a reporter of debates in Parliament for the *Morning Chronicle*. Dickens first achieved literary success at the age of 25 with the immensely popular *Pickwick Papers*. In speaking of *A Christmas Carol*, Charles Dickens said that he laughed and cried over it like he did over no other story.